michael morpurgo

Mudpuddle Farm

Hee-Haw Hooray!

Illustrated by Shoo Rayner

HarperCollins *Children's Books*

First published in Great Britain by HarperCollins Children's Books in 2017
HarperCollins Children's Books is a division of HarperCollins*Publishers* Ltd,
1 London Bridge Street, London, SE1 9GF

The HarperCollins website address is: www.harpercollins.co.uk

1

Text copyright © Michael Morpurgo 2017
Illustrations copyright © Shoo Rayner 2017

ISBN: 978–00–0–824198–8

Michael Morpurgo and Shoo Rayner assert the moral right to be identified as the
author and illustrator of the work.

Printed and bound in England by Clays Ltd, St Ives plc

MIX
Paper from
responsible sources
FSC® C007454

FSC™ is a non-profit international organisation established to promote
the responsible management of the world's forests. Products carrying the
FSC label are independently certified to assure consumers that they come
from forests that are managed to meet the social, economic and
ecological needs of present and future generations,
and other controlled sources.

Find out more about HarperCollins and the environment at
www.harpercollins.co.uk/green

Join the fun on
Mudpuddle Farm

Hee-Haw Hooray!

Books by Michael Morpurgo

For Bethany,
and all the children who come to
Farms for City Children at Nethercott – M. M.

For Molly Rae – S. R.

Contents

Mudpuddle Farm

Nowt to worry About

Chapter One

There was once a family of all sorts of animals that lived in the farmyard behind the tumbledown barn on Mudpuddle Farm.

At first light every morning, Frederick
the flame-feathered cockerel lifted his
eyes to the sun and crowed and crowed
and crowed until the light came on in
old Farmer Rafferty's bedroom window.

One by one the animals crept out into

the dawn, and yawned, and stretched,

and scratched themselves. But no one

spoke a word, not until after breakfast.

'Funny,' said Captain, Farmer Rafferty's great big carthorse whom everyone loved and who loved everyone, 'I don't think I like the look of that sky at all, nor the sound of it neither, not one bit.'

Mossop, the farm cat with the one and single eye, lay curled up in his usual place on the tractor seat. He was only half awake. 'Same sky as yesterday, Captain,' he said sleepily, 'same sky as always. And you can't hear the sky. You worry too much. Nowt to worry about.' And he went back to sleep again. He was so fast asleep he didn't hear a peep, didn't notice a thing.

15

Peggoty, the big pink pig, was snuffling about the farmyard with her ten little piglets when she heard it too. She looked up at the sky. 'I don't like the look of that sky at all,' she said. 'Nor the sound of it.'

Come along inside the barn, my lovelies. We can snuffle about in there. Nowt to worry about.

I want to go wee-wee, all the way home.

'I'm telling you, Mossop,' said Captain,
'that sky's not right.'

But Mossop wasn't listening. He was still fast asleep on his tractor seat, catching mice in his dreams. It was the only place he could catch them these days.

Just then, out of the farmhouse came old Farmer Rafferty, singing away as usual. He loved to sing while he worked, or to whistle. It kept him happy, kept all the farm animals happy too. Usually.

I like to sing my happy little song.

Sing, sing, sing, all day long.

He can't hear it.

'Good morning, Captain, my dear,' he said as he fed him his hay. But Captain wasn't at all interested in his breakfast, which old Farmer Rafferty thought was most unusual.

'I don't like the look of that sky, Mr Rafferty,' said Captain.

Merrily, merrily. Tiddly pom. I like to sing my happy song!

But old Farmer Rafferty wasn't listening – he was singing too loudly – and anyway he was getting a bit deaf these days. He just went on with feeding all the animals, singing and whistling as he worked.

He was singing while he milked the cows in the barn, first Aunty Grace the dreamy-eyed brown cow, and then Primrose, who always agreed with her. 'You give me more milk if I sing to you, if you're happy. Right, my dears? And that means more butter and more cheese.'

I am **nineteen** going on **twenty-one!**

'I like Adele best,'
said Aunty Grace,
her ears twitching.
'Or the Beatles
or Beethoven.'

'Me too,'
Primrose agreed.

I like any kind
of moosic!

COWS!

They let down their milk for him, all they had. But that wasn't much this morning, no matter which songs Farmer Rafferty was singing. And they were whisking their tails a lot, not at all happy. And, just like Captain, they didn't want to eat their hay either. They were upset about something, but old Farmer Rafferty didn't know what it was.

He patted their necks, and stroked them gently. 'Nowt to worry about, my dears. Nowt to worry about.'

He whistled when he went out to feed the hens, amongst them his favourite, Penelope, and her twelve little fluffy chicks. 'When you're a happy hen, you lay me an egg every day, Penelope, my dear, don't you?' And he bent down to look in her laying box.

NO EGGS TODAY

And it was true: every day Penelope would lay him another lovely brown egg. But not this morning. No egg was there today. And she was not eating her corn either – none of the hens were. He could tell they weren't at all happy no matter what tune he whistled, but didn't know why. He thought it might be the fox that was worrying Penelope.

'Nowt to worry about, my dear. Nowt to worry about. Old Mr Fox won't hurt you or your little chicks. I'll look after you. I'll see to that.'

GRUMBLE!

But it wasn't long before old Farmer Rafferty realised that it wasn't just the hens that were off their food. None of the animals seemed to want to eat their breakfast this morning.

'What is up with them all?' Farmer Rafferty asked himself out loud, scratching his head. 'They've all got twitchy ears or twitchy tails. Not happy, none of them. And they're gathering in the barn, huddling together, and that's not like them. Something's wrong.'

Whiiiish!

Jigger, the almost-always-sensible
sheepdog who usually liked to be off
on his own, running about the farm if
he could, was staying close to Farmer
Rafferty's side, his nose almost glued to
Farmer Rafferty's leg, his ears and eyes
going this way and that. He was shaking
all over.

Upside and Down, the two ducks, were upside down in the pond as usual, but their tail feathers were trembling.

On the island in the pond, Albertine the clever goose hid her eight little goslings under her feathers, and her head too. She was upset as well.

Then Farmer Rafferty saw that even Egberta the goat and her two little kids weren't eating, and Egberta was always eating, eating anything:

paper sacks

socks off the washing line

newspapers

anything.

But not this morning. Egberta and her little kids just stood there in the corner of the barn, all miserable and sad, hiding their heads.

Frederick the flame-feathered cockerel was there too by now, crestfallen, his wings drooping, not happy at all.

And all the sheep and lambs were
huddled together, heads in the haystack.

Old Farmer Rafferty couldn't see them,
but all the mice and rats were hiding away
down in their holes, every one of them.

And the family of barn owls were sitting high up on their perches, close together to comfort one another, and the swallows had also come inside,

too many to count, and they were lined
up side by side on the beam, wings
around one another, all of them wishing
they were far away in Africa.

'What is the matter with you all?' cried old Farmer Rafferty.

There's nowt to worry about, my dears!

Poor old Farmer Rafferty, he still couldn't hear what Aunty Grace and Primrose could hear,

and Peggoty and all the little piglets could hear,

and Penelope and her chicks could hear,

what Jigger could hear,
what the sheep and

the lambs
could hear,

the owls and the swallows too,

and Egberta,
and her kids,

what Frederick the flame-feathered
cockerel could hear,

what they could all hear now. All except
poor old Farmer Rafferty.

RUMBLE!

I hear
NOTHING!

Thunder! Thunder grumbling and growling, rumbling and rolling around the hills in the distance and coming closer all the time.

CLOSER

CLO

But then it got so close that old Farmer
Rafferty did hear it at last. 'Nowt to
worry about, my dears,' he said.
'Just one of those little thunderstorms.
It'll pass. They always do.'

RUMBLE
GRUMBLE

He whistled
a tune to try
to make them
happier, but it didn't.

I'm not scared.
Nothing scares me.
A little bit of thunder
never bothered me.

He sang
a song.
That didn't
work either.

The sheep were bleating, the goats too.

Jigger was whining and barking.

Peggoty and her little piglets were squealing.

The hens were squawking.

Squ-a-a-r-k!

The cows were mooing.

MOO!

The owls screeched and the swallows twittered.

Screeech!

And Captain was neighing loudly from his stable.

'I'd best go and fetch Captain,' said old Farmer Rafferty. 'He's all on his own in the stable. He sounds a bit upset.' And off he went.

Wheeesh!

Zooosh!

Whooosh!

Outside the wind was howling, blowing the clouds and the crows and the leaves across the sky, whipping the branches about, shaking and rattling the windows and doors of the farmhouse, of the farm buildings all around. Old Farmer Rafferty could hardly walk across the yard. The wind was trying to blow him off his feet! And the rain was coming down so hard it stung his face.

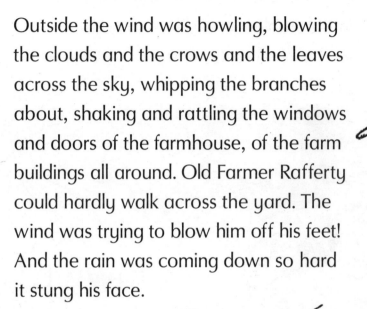

And, in fact, it was the wind that woke Mossop up at last, and almost blew him off his tractor seat. He was scared stiff of the wind and hated getting wet, so he scampered as quickly as he could into the barn to get out of the rain and to be with the others.

Old Farmer Rafferty was just leading Captain across the farmyard towards the barn when it happened. There was a great crash of thunder overhead, and then a crackle and crack of lightning that lit up the whole sky.

'It's nowt to worry about, Captain, my dear!' he shouted. 'Just a bit of a storm. You come along with me into the barn and join the others.'

Nowt to worry about!

Just then there came another great
crackle and crack of lightning, and then
a thunderbolt struck the roof of the barn.
At once the roof burst into flames, little
ones at first, but very soon the wind
had whipped the fire up and it was
spreading fast, roaring, raging.

Old Farmer Rafferty didn't run much these days but he did now. 'Fire, fire!' he cried, and he ran as fast as his old legs could carry him across the farmyard and into the barn.

'Out you come, my dears,' he told them,
'nice and slow now, no panic. Nowt to
worry about. Keep calm, my dears.'

And out of the barn they came. They stood in the farmyard in the pouring rain, dripping wet, sad to see their barn burning, but happy to be alive.

The fire engines came as quickly as they could. They did their best, but they could not put out the fire, could not save the barn, nor Captain's stable.

Smoke

Smoulder

Old Farmer Rafferty did not mind so much about the barn or the stable; he just wanted to be sure that all the animals were safe and sound. So he kept counting them again and again, just to be sure all of them were there, all the sheep, all the hens, the cows, the goats – all of them – and they were.

'I can build a new barn, my dears,' he said, 'and I will.'

All that matters, my dears, is that no one is missing and none of us has been hurt.

'Mr Rafferty,' said Captain, after it was all over.

And all the animals agreed, except
Upside and Down who were still upside
down in the pond.

With the thunder gone now, Albertine the clever goose lifted her head out from under her feathers at last and looked about her. 'I'm glad everyone is all right,' she said.

You should live on an island with water all around – **much** safer.

Now Farmer Rafferty can't build a barn in a day, or a week, or even a month, can he? Without the barn, where are you all going to live now? I can live on my pond, so can Upside and Down. But what about you? Where will he milk the cows? And without a stable where is Captain going to live? Have you thought of that?

She's the BEST mum in the world.

She's SO clever.

And of course no one had. They all looked at one another. They all looked very worried. And they were all looking at old Farmer Rafferty.

Old Farmer Rafferty thought for a while, a long while. His ideas came more slowly to him these days. 'Nowt to worry about, my dears,' he said at last.

You shall all come and sleep in my house till we can build the barn again. Nice and warm in there. Plenty of room for all of us, and I like a bit of company. How would that be, my dears?

So that's what happened, from that very evening. The farmhouse had never been so full, nor so happy. Only Mossop wasn't pleased. When he wasn't sleeping on his tractor seat outside, he was quite happy to share the house with old Farmer Rafferty, and he was used to that.

I'm a guest!

But to share it with all these hens and sheep and cows and goats and pigs and owls and swallows, and Captain too, well, that was a bit much. Even the mice and rats had been invited in!

Old Farmer Rafferty could see Mossop was a bit put out, so he took him up to bed with him and they snuggled down together.

The night came down, the moon came up
and everyone slept on Mudpuddle Farm.

Mudpuddle Farm

Tickety-BOO

Captain

Chapter One

There was once a family of all sorts
of animals that lived in the farmyard
down on Mudpuddle Farm. At first light
every morning, Frederick the flame-
feathered cockerel crowed and crowed
and crowed until the light came on in old
Farmer Rafferty's bedroom window.

One by one the animals crept out into

the dawn, and stretched and yawned, and

scratched themselves. But no one spoke

a word, not until after breakfast.

Summer had come again to Mudpuddle Farm, so most of the animals were outside, grazing happily in the fields. They all loved the summertime. Old Farmer Rafferty did too.

He loved to see the green of the grass,

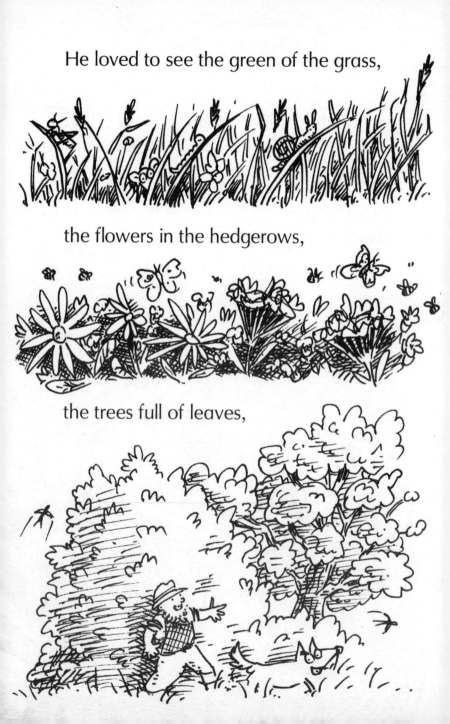

the flowers in the hedgerows,

the trees full of leaves,

swallows swooping over the fields,

bees buzzing in the orchard

and the corn growing high.

And he didn't have to work so hard either,
because the cows and calves, and pigs
and goats, and all his sheep and hens,
and dear old Captain, the farm horse, lived
outdoors in the summer, so he didn't have

to feed them. They fed themselves and looked after themselves, mostly. He didn't have to clean out their barns and sheds and stables any more either. So old Farmer Rafferty was a happy man.

All he had to do every morning was to
get up slowly,

have a nice long breakfast,

open up the henhouse for Penelope and
her twelve little chicks,

then milk Aunty Grace the dreamy-eyed brown cow, and Primrose who always agreed with her.

And that's what he was doing this fine summer morning.

He had just finished the milking, just taken Aunty Grace and Primrose back into their field ...

WHEN ...

he suddenly heard an almighty kerfuffle going on out in the farm.

Jigger was barking his head off. The sheep were scattering across the fields, baaing their heads off. Upside and Down had flown off the pond and were quacking their heads off as they flew over Farmer Rafferty's head. Penelope was running around clucking her head off, Frederick

was crowing his head off and the little chicks were cheeping their heads off. Peggoty and all her little piglets were squealing their heads off. Albertine was honking her head off too from her island in the middle of the pond, all her little goslings hiding their heads away underneath her wings.

Of course Mossop was fast asleep as usual on his tractor seat, chasing mice in his dreams. So he didn't hear what the animals had, what old Farmer Rafferty was now hearing – even if he couldn't hear quite so well these days.

It wasn't a bleating or a snorting.

BAAAA!

OINK!

It wasn't a mooing,

MOOOOO!

a clucking

CLUCK!

SQUEAL!

or a squealing

or even a neighing.

NEI-I-I-IGH!

It was all of these put together, a sort of moo-snorty, squeal-clucky, neigh-bleaty sound, unlike anything they had ever heard before, a sound that seemed to wind itself up and then echo out over the fields, before stopping for a moment and winding itself up again. A truly dreadful noise!

MOO-SNORTY,

SQUEAL,

And now Aunty Grace and Primrose were mooing their heads off too, and running away down the hill. Running! Aunty Grace and Primrose were running!

That was when old Farmer Rafferty
really knew something must be wrong.
All the animals were running down the
hill now towards the stream.

Old Farmer Rafferty couldn't really run
– he was far too old for that – but he
did break into a trot as he made his way
down the hill to see what was going on,
what all the kerfuffle was about.

And that's when he saw the most extraordinary sight. He could not believe his eyes. Captain was trotting over the bridge neighing his head off. And on the other side of the stream stood ... what could it be?

Like a horse
but not as big
as a horse.

Like a zebra,
but with no
stripes.

Like a deer,
but shaggier
and with
big ears.

What was it?

Chapter Four

'Captain's had a baby!'
clucked Penelope
excitedly.

'So he has!'
snorted Peggoty.

'Don't think so,' said Albertine, who was
always right about everything. 'That is a
donkey. Look at his ears. Listen to his voice.'

Baa!

Captain was trotting right up to the
donkey, and the two of them tossed
heads at one another in a friendly sort
of a way, touched noses and then,
after some gentle snuffling and neck

scratching, the two of them wandered off together up the hill on the other side of the stream and began grazing the grass side by side as if they had been friends all their lives.

It took a while for old Farmer Rafferty to catch up with them. He was puffed out by the time he did.

Where did your friend come from, then, Captain, my dear? Nice old donkey. Hello, old fellow, have a carrot. I've always got carrots in my pocket; all my animals like carrots and so do I.

And then, as Captain and his new friend and old Farmer Rafferty chomped happily away on their carrots, a voice called out to them from the wood at the top of the hill. An old lady with a stick came tottering down across the field.

'Hopalong! Hopalong!' she cried.

'No harm done, Miss Brightwell. You take him home and I'll shut Captain in for a while,' said old Farmer Rafferty, leading Captain away. Or trying to. And, when Miss Brightwell tried to lead the donkey away, he didn't want to go either.

In the end Farmer Rafferty had to use up all the carrots in his pockets to tempt them away from one another.

The animals all stood there, watching, not at all pleased that Captain and his new donkey friend were getting all those nice juicy carrots.

Chapter Five

Captain was led away back to his stable
and shut in. He was not at all a happy
horse. He kept neighing and kicking at
his water bucket, kicking at the door,
no matter how many carrots he got. In
fact, he was so upset he wouldn't even
eat them now.

I'll
have it!

He stood there in the stable hour after hour, hanging his head, looking very miserable. Nothing would cheer him up:

not
Mossop
singing
to him,
not even
old Farmer
Rafferty's
sweetest
hay.

All the animals came to visit him because they hated to see him so unhappy. They all knew he was missing his new friend, but nothing they did or said seemed to cheer him up.

And the next morning, when old Farmer Rafferty went out to give him his hay in his stable, what did he find? There was Hopalong the donkey in the stable yard, nose to nose with Captain, both of them as happy as you like.

Soon enough Miss Brightwell came over again to fetch him home. But Hopalong didn't want to go home.

He brayed and he brayed –

BREE-HAW

what a dreadful racket he made! –

HEE-HAW!

and he would not budge …

not even for carrots.

In the end they gave up trying – much to the animals' delight because at last the dreadful braying stopped. They led them both out into the field, where they wandered off together quite happily.

Old Farmer Rafferty and old Miss Brightwell leant on the gate, watching them, trying to work out what to do, how to get Hopalong to leave Captain or Captain to leave Hopalong.

Egberta the always-greedy goat
chewed at the back of Miss Brightwell's
coat because she liked coats. Coats
tasted delicious. Miss Brightwell didn't
seem to mind.

Behind them, all the animals looked on, wondering what was going to happen.

Out on the pond Albertine the goose was thinking deep goosey thoughts. Upside and Down, the two ducks, turned upside down in the pond, and Mossop jumped up on to his tractor seat to go to sleep again.

Glub ...

Blub ...

'I think there is only one way to solve this,' said Albertine to her little gosling children. 'Old Farmer Rafferty is going to have to learn to think laterally.'

'Yes, Mum,' they piped. 'Laterally sounds an excellent idea ... What does it mean?'

'You will see, children, you will see,' she told them wisely. And then she honked loudly and often, until old Farmer Rafferty turned round to see what the matter was. She looked at him, and he looked at her.

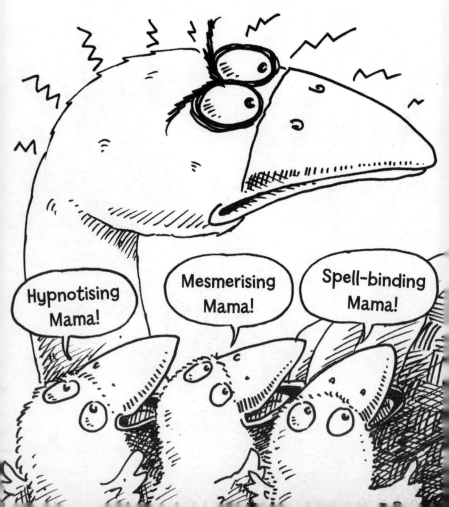

She spoke to him with her eyes: that's all Albertine had to do. He understood exactly what she was trying to tell him.

'Do you know, Miss Brightwell,' he began, 'I do believe that goose of mine is a genius!'

We know that.

She should get a Nobel Prize!

And then, with a wink at Albertine, he went on. 'Would you like to come inside the farmhouse for a nice cup of tea, Miss Brightwell?'

Miss Brightwell looked rather puzzled,
but off they went into the house,
Egberta still chewing on her coat.

Outside, all the animals gathered to see what would happen, how old Farmer Rafferty and Miss Brightwell were going to find a way to separate Captain and Hopalong.

Chapter Seven

'Miss Brightwell,' began old Farmer
Rafferty, as they sat down for tea and
cake in the kitchen, 'we have a problem,
you and me, and Hopalong and
Captain. You live in the village; I live

here. Hopalong lives in the village; dear old Captain lives here on the farm. Even if we manage to part those two, old Hopalong will find his way back here again.'

'True enough, Mr Rafferty,' she replied.

'Well, we thought – I thought – that maybe Hopalong could stay here for a while, come for a bit of a holiday,' he said, 'and you could visit him whenever you like, have a cup of tea like this and a piece of cake. And they'd be tickety-boo and we'd be tickety-boo and everything would be tickety-boo. What do you say?'

she said, eating her cake, and wrinkling
her nose at it a bit. 'But on one
condition. That I bake a nice cake – a
nicer cake than this one – and bring it
with me.'

When they came out of the farmhouse, the animals were all waiting to hear the news. 'It's all right, my dears,' old Farmer Rafferty said. 'Hopalong and Captain can stay together. For now, anyway. And Miss Brightwell will come to visit him and you and me, here on the farm, whenever and as often as she wishes.'

Off they went to tell Captain and Hopalong, who galloped away together around the field, neighing and nickering and braying, because that's what that moo-snorty, squeal-clucky, neigh-bleaty sound is called. They were so happy.

Chapter Eight

As Jigger came padding back that evening from chasing rabbits, he saw Albertine sitting on her island with her little gosling children. 'Heard the glad news about that Hopalong and Captain?' he said.

'I don't *hear* news, Jigger,' she told him.

And she was right, of course. Miss Brightwell came visiting every day, every week, every month, until she and old

Farmer Rafferty gathered all the animals together one evening in front of the farmhouse.

'I have happy news for you, my dears,' she said. 'I have asked Mr Rafferty to marry me, and I am glad to tell you that he said yes. But he also said, "If you marry me, you marry my animals. Deal or no deal?" And I said to Mr Rafferty, "Deal!" And he said, "Tickety-boo!"'

And all the animals were so happy, Captain and Hopalong most of all, of course. And Hopalong celebrated with the loudest, longest, moo-snorty, squeal-clucky, neigh-bleaty braying he had ever done in all his life, until all the animals

SNICKER

SNORT

– except Captain of course – could not stand it any more and crept away into the darkening evening.

HEE-HAW!

The sun went down, the moon came up and everyone slept on Mudpuddle Farm.

Martians at Mudpuddle Farm

Have Martians landed on Mudpuddle Farm?
Farmer Rafferty seems to think so! It looks like an
alien invasion, and in a situation like that there's
only one animal to turn to - Albertine, the
cleverest goose in the world ...

Mum's the word

Something strange is going on - instead of grumbling,
Egbert the goat is singing and dancing! And he's even
greedier than usual. But why doesn't Farmer Rafferty
complain when Egbert eats all his carrots?
As always, Albertine has an idea ...